The Gay Icon Classics Of The World II

Robert Joseph Greene

ISBN: 469914158
ISBN 13: 9781469914152

published by :

ICON EMPIRE PRESS

552 Church Street Toronto, ON

M4Y 2E3 CANADA.

NOTICE

All characters appearing in this work are fictitious. Any resemblance to any real persons, living or dead, is purely coincidental.

CONTENTS

Introduction

1. The Dalit Boy (India)   1

2. The Laughing Brothers (Korea)   13

3. The Red Rheum (China)   23

4. The Game Of Nard (Persia-Iran)   45

5. The Kuri Village (Australia)   57

6. Tukkuruq and Uquitchuq: The Story Of Night And Day (Canada)   67

7. The Blue Door (Russia)   77

8. The Pink Tie Dance (Argentina)   83

ACKNOWLEDGMENTS

I would like to thank Rev. Marguerite Lovett, Rabbi Stephen Greenberg, Dan Mohan, Camilla Greene, Catherine Adamson for their proofreading and editing and/or moral support.

1 THE DALIT BOY(INDIA)

The story of Mizra Daksha and Anurag: How Love Came To India.

Once upon a time, the great ancient Zamindar clans ruled the Eastern lands of India, where the great Ganges River meets her smaller cousins the Son, Gandak, and Kosi. In these fertile lands lived a prince named Mizra Daksha. His father, Mehar, was a great raja, and his family ruled over vast estates in Eastern Bihar.

Growing up, Mizra loved everything his family's vast land had to offer. He loved the holy temples that were decorated with intricate sculptures of saints and sinners, telling tales of good triumphing over evil. These stories occupied Mizra's childhood, providing him with dreams of a more romantic time, a time that seemed more just and pure. The Mahabodhi Temple was his favorite temple, and he would spend the evenings running about its grounds. It towered magnificently over the village. Mizra's uncle Naleda would tell him stories of how Buddha himself achieved enlightenment under the Bodhi tree next to the temple. The Bodhi tree was a sacred tree, and the temple was built in homage to Buddha's enlightenment.

"Sometimes certain paths are not made by man himself," Naleda would say, "but rather the path is destined, especially in matters of the heart." Mizra often pondered his uncle's replies to his often repetitive questions.

Mizra's father, Raja Mehar, and his mother, Yesubai, were keen for him to become the next Raja of Bihar. His father wanted him to rule as he did, with constant stern strength over the lower clans of Bihar.

"There are those who rule and those who are to be ruled," the raja would always say.

His mother, also from a long line of proud Zamindars, wanted Mizra to maintain their clan's rule over Bihar.

"You are a Zamindar. That is who we are and who we will always be. We are made to rule," she would say.

His life was a constant routine with every aspect laid out for him. He had everything he needed and wanted in life. He had servants to bathe him, to choose his clothes, to shield him from the sun, to fan him, even to taste his food. Mizra also had advisors and oracles to tell his future. Like so many princes next in line to a throne, Mizra accepted his fate. However, he always felt that his family's status contradicted the teachings of Buddha.

"I guess enlightenment is only for the privileged," he would reluctantly think to himself.

Mizra's privileged life gave him a sense of aimlessness. He soon got into the habit of wandering the streets around the palace, tailed unerringly by his servants. One day, however, he tricked two of his servants who were watching him. He dashed through a small alleyway after requesting his servants purchase a Honey Buzzard for him. The alleyway he passed through housed a community of Dalits, who stared at him as he dashed through.

As Mizra reached the end of the alley and stopped to catch his breath, he was approached by one of the Dalits. A boy clad in a tattered brown robe with patches of mud on his face and legs asked for a few coins. Mizra, a little scared because it was his first time encountering a Dalit, ignored him and walked away.

The boy followed him, hoping he would change his mind. Seeing this, Mizra began sprinting again, but the boy matched his pace.

Mizra Daksha ran so fast that he lost his balance and tripped into a drainage ditch that was filled with water. Under the dead leaves and branches, Mizra gasped for breath. If there was one thing that was not part of his royal routines, it was learning how to swim. The Dalit boy dove to his rescue. He pulled an unconscious Mizra out of the ditch.

Mizra gazed at the boy's face. The mud stains had washed off. He stripped off his robe, which revealed his lanky, small-framed body. The boy was shaking his head and stood with his arms crossed, as if Mizra had done something completely silly and clueless.

"Why are you grinning at me? What is your name, boy?" asked Mizra.

"My name! Ahhh, you think I have a name? We are all the same to your kind. Dalit. That is my name. You saw me as a Dalit just now, and you probably still see me as one. You want to know my name? Why, so you can thank me? You're welcome," the boy replied sarcastically.

"I'm sorry I ran away. I was a little scared."

"Scared?" the boy replied. "You could have just said no."

"Why did you save me?"

"Because the teachings of Buddha tell us to respect every human life." With those words, the Dalit boy simply walked away.

As soon as Mizra returned to the palace, his mother shouted at him for returning home so late.

"Where have you been? Why are you soaking wet? You always wander off and don't think about your responsibilities!" she screeched. "Especially on the day that we found you a bride, Princess Sweetha from the kingdom of Nepal. She is a darling. Many have tried to win her hand, but no one can say no to your father, my dear," said Yesubai.

Mizra was shocked, considering the events that had just transpired. His mother embraced him, but deep inside his mind, Mizra was overwhelmed.

As the days went by, the only place Mizra was permitted to stroll was to the Mahabodhi temple. His parents placed more servants around Mizra in case he went missing again. The palace was abuzz with preparations to announce his engagement, but all Mizra could think about was the Dalit boy. He knew his parents loved him, but he couldn't help wondering why he felt an emotional connection to the humble act of that young Dalit.

As the great day for his family dawned, Mizra Daksha approached his father the raja and asked if he could postpone this announcement until Mizra had cleared his head. The raja said no and told his son that he knew what was best for him. His mother gave him the same response.

Mizra didn't want this life. His destiny and the way things were in Bihar had been fed to him since childhood. He wanted to learn things beyond ruling and palace life. He wanted to learn selflessness, and he wanted to learn love. If he had a quest like Buddha, it would be for love.

Mizra managed to slip out of the palace during the night after the guards had dozed off out of boredom. He returned to the alleyway and asked around for the Dalit boy. Every resident in the slum houses said he didn't live there. As Mizra approached the end of the alleyway, there the Dalit boy stood, asking him for a few coins. This time Mizra obliged.

"I want to live with you, but I don't know why. Where do you live?" Mizra begged.

"Where I live, they come without being fetched. By day they are lost without being stolen. So where can this place be?"

Mizra realized with shame the answer to the boy's riddle. "You have no home. You live under the stars. If it is under the stars that you live, then under the stars I shall too." With those words, he tore off his clothes, wrapped himself in a simple loincloth, and joined the Dalit boy.

It took him some time to adapt to life as a beggar, but it suited Mizra well.

On his first day, he knelt next to the boy and began to beg.

"Don't be so silly," said the boy, smiling at Mizra's foolishness. "They won't give to us both. You must stake out another place."

"All right," said Mizra, and he got up and stationed himself across the street within direct view of the boy.

At first, Mizra had a tough time begging, but soon he figured a great trick for getting people's attention.

"You sir," he would say.

"Go away, beggar."

"I have something for you. Perhaps you are interested?"

"Ha, you have nothing…What is it?"

"I know something that is all about but cannot be seen. Can be captured, cannot be held. No throat, but can be heard.…Do you know what it is?"

Amused, the stranger replied, "No."

"Why, it is the wind, of course!" said Mizra. "See now I did give you something; I gave you knowledge. However, if you add that you laughed, I gave you two things."

"That you did. Here." The stranger tossed him a gold coin.

"Thank you, kind sir. If you return again, I will say something different."

The stranger walked off, laughing to himself. A while later he returned with a friend.

"OK, I have brought you a scholar. Lay your words on him."

"OK, but what if he does not know the answer? There are two of you and one of me; that makes three. So may I get six gold coins?"

By now a crowd had formed. The Dalit boy wondered why but didn't bother to move because he figured people realized that Mizra was being silly.

When the day ended, the prince crossed the street and gathered his young companion. They went to fetch food with the many coins Mizra had acquired.

"I got it from your words, my dear."

"Don't be silly. You got nothing from me."

"That is not true. You saved my life; that is something. But eat now! Let us enjoy this food"

"OK," said the boy.

"Tell me your favorite fruit, and I shall buy it. Tell me your favorite vegetable, and you shall have it," said Mizra.

The boy had never been offered such a treat.

Both nourished and happy, the Dalit boy turned to Mizra and said, "OK, so I saved your life. But it was really nothing because I am sure you would have done the same for me."

Mizra looked down and said, "Because of the things that have influenced my life, I am sadly ashamed to say that I would not have."

"So you gave me food. What can I give you?"

"You already gave it to me, but if you answer my riddle, you will see clearer."

If you break me,

I do not stop working. If you touch me,

I may be snared.

If you lose me, nothing will matter.

"My heart?" said the boy.

And with that answer Mizra kissed the young Dalit boy.

The Dalit boy smiled because the sensation from the kiss brought back long-forgotten feelings deep inside, feelings he had only experienced for brief moments, if not seconds, in his life.

That night they lay together, and in the morning the boy said, "Yes, I do have something to give you."

"What is it?"

"My name…I just remembered it. It's Anurag. I had no reason to give it to anyone, and therefore I forgot it. But it came to me because of you."

Mizra was in a state of bliss upon hearing these words.

Meanwhile at the palace, Yesubai grew concerned because her son, who was known to wander for days, hadn't returned in weeks. The bride was set to arrive for the wedding any day now. The raja sent his guards to look for his son, but they came back without him.

"Oh, he is just hiding. He will appear," said the raja.

However, the day of the wedding arrived, and still their son, Mizra Daksha, had not returned. Crowds had formed to see their raja and the royal family. Yesubai spotted a young lad among the Dalit beggars who she was certain was her son. He seemed a bit gaunt and dirty, but she was certain it was him. So she approached him and said, "Mizra Daksha, how could you let yourself become so dirty and be among these Dalits when your future wife shall appear so soon?"

The young man stared blankly at the woman. "Is your name Mizra Daksha?"

He shook his head.

"What is your name then?"

"Dalit," he replied.

"That is not your name. You're stupid. That is the name of your people."

"It is indeed my name because you don't see any of us, so seeing one of us makes no difference," he said.

Yesubai walked away almost certain that he was not her son because no son of hers would ever say such silly words. Mizra Daksha went back into the crowd and joined Anurag, happy and in love. Enlightenment had come to this land a long time ago, but true love had just sprung to life.

2 THE LAUGHING BROTHERS (KOREA)

Not long ago, just over a hill, lived a mother and her two sons, Hyo and Shin.

They loved each other very much, each in their own fashion. The mother looked after the house, the farm, and the boys with perhaps more worry than necessary. Whatever she did, she wore a constant frown. The boys looked after each other in all the ways good brothers should. They did their chores together, worked together, and played together.

They were also scolded together. Their mother would scold them for things they did and things they didn't do, for the things they did wrong and the things they did right. She would always find something mean to say to Hyo and Shin, though she loved them all the same. Some mothers just need to nag and pick and poke, you see.

The boys learned early in life that the best response to that sort of meanness was to laugh. The brothers were both brilliant and beautiful laughers. If you heard either of them laughing, you would start laughing yourself, and if you heard both of them laughing at the same time, you would fill up with so much warmth that it would melt even the memory of the cold. Their mother listened to them laughing all day long and just frowned all the harder.

Best of all, the boys loved contradicting their mother. She would tell them, "Be sure to get up early!" and they would be sure to get up late. She would tell them, "Be sure to clean your bowls after supper!" and they would leave their bowls unwashed. Sometimes she would say, "Let me do the washing up," and before she could turn around, the brothers had done all the cleaning. They weren't bad boys, you see, just very contradictory. Every time they contradicted their mother and she would begin to scold them, they would say something they remembered their father saying: "To know if it's a bad thing or good, you have to wait awhile." Then they would laugh together, long and deep laughs, right from their bellies.

Time went by, and the boys became young men, as boys have a habit of doing. One day their mother was feeling especially frustrated with their contradictions and all of their laughing. She said to them, "Go away and find wives! Find some other women to put up with your jokes and contradictions, and I will give you each a share of this land for your own farm." The brothers heard this, looked each other in the eye, and grinned, for they already knew how they would contradict their mother's demand.

Hyo and Shin talked late into the night, planning and packing for their journey. They set out just before dawn, joking and laughing along the road before going their separate ways. Their mother waited a day for them to come back, and then a week. By two weeks, she missed them a little. By three weeks, she One month after her sons had left home, she looked down the road and felt her heart jump in her chest. An ox cart with both sons on the back was rolling down the road toward her, and she could see the silhouettes of two other passengers with them. The thought that her sons had finally conceded to her demands filled her with so much joy that her frown almost slipped.

"Mother, mother!" called Shin.

"We've brought our brides!" called Hyo.

As the cart drew near, she began to suspect that her sons had not given up their habit of contradiction. Hyo grinned a broad, mischievous grin, and Shin smiled shyly as if keeping a secret. Their brides' faces were both covered in silk scarves. They stopped the cart in front of the house. The brothers clambered out, greeting their mother with hugs and kisses on the cheek.

"Let us introduce our brides!" Hyo said, pulling the silk scarves off their heads.

When the scarves came off, she could hardly believe her eyes. The brothers' brides were men! Beautiful, smiling, and definitely men.

"This is my bride, Jung-Su," said Hyo.

"This is my beloved Dak-Ho," said Shin.

The look on their mother's face soured the milk inside the cow three farms over, and the brothers began to laugh their right-from-the-belly laugh. They crowed, "To know if it's a bad thing or good, you have to wait awhile!" as their mother retreated into the house, slamming the door behind her.

After she had gone, Hyo drew Shin away from the cart and said, "This is our best joke yet!"

Shin said nothing, smiling at Hyo, a smile that softened as he looked back to Dak-Ho.

"Why aren't you laughing?" Hyo asked. "We really showed her this time."

"Then I will show her still. I will keep Dak-Ho, if he will have me."

"Come now, Shin. The joke is over."

"It was never a joke for me," said Shin, looking back to the cart and Dak-Ho's cool, calm eyes.

"Are you a fool?" chided Hyo. "The love of a man cannot make you happy. Don't take our contradiction game too far."

"Hyo, we have always done the opposite of what mother asked, and that has always brought us happiness. I am already happy with Dak-Ho, and I will continue to be."

Hyo tried and tried, but Shin would not change his mind. That evening Shin talked to their mother. She argued and scolded and frowned as hard as she could, but seeing that Shin had made up his mind, she agreed to keep her end of the bargain and give Shin his share of the farm and its profits so he could build a home for himself and Dak-Ho.

The following morning Shin and Dak-Ho set off to their parcel of land to begin building their house. Hyo drove the cart to return Jung-Su to his home. When Hyo returned, he found his mother standing on the porch, smiling a smile more biting than her most terrible frown.

"It's just you and me now," she said, "and I'll have no more contradictions."

Sure enough, every time Hyo tried to contradict his mother or play a joke, he would turn to where he expected Shin to be and find he didn't have the heart to do it. From sunrise to sunset he listened to his mother's scolding and complaining, which seemed even worse than ever, even though he no longer contradicted her.

Hyo decided to find a proper wife so he could build his own home and get away from his mother, but she found ways to slip her scolding and demands into that too. He would bring a woman home, and his mother would say she was too clean or too dirty, too short or too tall, too loud or too quiet. When he finally found a wife his mother approved of, he was too worn down to notice that she had all the same traits as his mother. When he told his mother whom he intended to marry, she smiled and nodded knowingly.

Hyo's new wife could complain rain from a clear sky. While she complained, Hyo built their house. While she complained, he seeded their farm, raised their crops, fed their chickens, and began to look very, very tired, right down to his belly that used to be full of laughter.

When the weather started to get cold, Hyo's mother decided she did not want to spend winter alone. Hyo opened his door one morning to find her standing there, smiling, telling him she would be moving in with them. You can just imagine how long the days became and how full of scolding they were now that Hyo heard it from his mother and the wife who his mother had chosen for him. Before long, Hyo's tiredness spread—the chickens, the vegetables, even the house seemed to groan and sigh and creak.

Once a week Hyo would take a cart to the market. Whatever he sold, his wife said he sold it for too little. Whatever he bought, his mother said he paid too much. Even though he knew he would come home to the worst complaining, he enjoyed going to the market, if only to get a few hours of peace.

One evening the idea of driving the cart home seemed especially awful. Hyo looked down the road toward his house, his wife, and his mother, and let out a long, tired sigh. Just as the sigh's tail slipped out of his mouth, he felt the tickling of an idea: He wondered how Shin and Dak-Ho were doing. He'd meant to visit them before but never seemed to have the time. He looked down the road to his house, and then down the winding path to Shin's farm, and turned his cart in that direction.

What sights Hyo saw as he came to Shin's farm! The chickens clucking contentedly, roosters strutting as if in a New Year's parade, vegetables bursting from the ground as bright, colorful, and lush as one could hope for. Even the roof of Shin's cottage seemed bowed as if the house were about to laugh.

With lungs full of the smells of happy growing, Hyo knocked on the door, afraid that Shin would scold him for not visiting sooner. Shin's cry of surprise and joy as he opened the door reached deep into Hyo, right down to the belly, and woke the laughter that had been sleeping there all this time. The brothers squeezed each other tight and laughed together, long and hard. Dak-Ho gave Hyo a warm, deep smile and led them inside to have tea.

They talked and laughed and sang songs together, all three of them. Hyo told Shin about his troubles. Shin told Hyo of his happiness with Dak-Ho. The sun went down, and Hyo felt a pinch of dread in his belly, knowing he would have to go home to more complaining than ever before for being so late. Shin assured him he could visit any time.

As Hyo climbed into his cart, Shin called out, "To know if it's a bad thing or good, you have to wait awhile!"

"That is true, brother, and this is good," Hyo replied.

Shin and Dak-Ho continued to live happily together. Hyo endured the nagging of his wife and mother with a smile, knowing that every time he went to market, he could slip away to visit Shin and Dak-Ho to enjoy an evening of laughter and peace.

3 THE RED RHEUM (CHINA)

The war had been over for months, but pockets of revolutionaries were still crossing the land. Imperial warriors were dispatched to protect the innocent civilians, but they functioned more as agents to prevent the spread of the revolutionaries' dangerous ideals and actions.

Nanyue was one of the greatest warriors in all of Asia. Under his direction, the battle of the Ugasi plains had been won. He soon became known as Nanyue the Great. He was a legend throughout all the provinces. Nanyue was taller and more muscular than any other warrior. His skin was tanned and smooth from the sun. He had a handsome face with deep brown eyes that seemed to peer into one's very soul. He was a man about whom many words were spoken, but who himself spoke very little. He had many admirers but few friends.

Nanyue had been on his solitary trek across the Gobi Desert for almost two months when he reached the city of Jiauguan. It was here, Nanyue decided, that he would rest a few days and restock his supplies before moving on. It was dusk when he reached the city, and because he preferred to be alone, he made his camp on the city's outskirts near a gathering of trees.

Rei had lived just outside of Jiauguan all of his life, raised by a peasant farmer to be an obedient child. Rei was also a cheerful child, but his parents believed boys should not be emotional. Rei would dream fondly of a life different from his own. He would gaze longingly at the infrequent warriors who passed through the city, imagining the life they led and the things they had seen. His father would scold him for daydreaming when he should have been working, but Rei could not help but to imagine the glamorous life of a warrior.

Work started at dawn for Rei, and this morning when he stepped into the field, rubbing the sleep from his eyes, he was surprised to see a camp just inside the field boundary. The setup indicated that an imperial warrior was dwelling there, but work on the farm was an all-day task, so Rei would not have time to investigate until later. The morning passed, and Rei ached with excitement and anticipation. But when mealtime came, Rei went to the stranger's camp instead. The stranger's armor made it clear that the he was indeed an Imperial warrior. Upon sight of the stranger's face, Rei knew this was Nanyue the Great. Rei had believed the warrior's appearance had been exaggerated, but he quickly saw that he had been wrong.

Rei caught Nanyue in the midst of filling his water bag in a small pond, so he spoke with no real thought or restraint.

"If you are the honorable Nanyue, please allow me to carry those for you." Rei held his hands out and bowed, hoping his offer would be accepted.

Nanyue studied the boy for a moment, and then passed him the water bags and gestured with his hand to indicate the direction they would be going. Several minutes of silence passed as they walked. Then Rei spoke.

"You are Nanyue the Great, are you not?" Rei spoke quickly and a little fearfully.

"Perhaps," replied Nanyue, not looking away from the road.

"I have heard so much about you, tales of your deeds. I am fortunate to assist one such as you, a warrior from the honorable Imperial Guard."

Nanyue looked at Rei once before turning his eyes back to the road.

Rei felt a bit smug at the thought of what the city folk would think when they saw him in the company of this great warrior. As Nanyue entered the house, Rei once again acted with no real thought or hesitation.

"If you would care for any assistance at all, I am at your service." Rei blushed a little at his own boldness, but kept his voice and eyes steady, hope tugging at his heart. But Nanyue said nothing as he disappeared. Rei waited.

The interior of the building was cool and dim, the floor made of highly polished wood and the walls decorated with large silk drapes of purple. Nanyue did not stop to appreciate the silk screens and bronze statuettes that dotted the room but went directly to the house officials and presented them a note. The officials sat at a long table in awe at being in the presence of the warrior. One official took the note with trembling hands and shared it with the others; the note entitled the warrior to a rather large payment from the Imperial House.

"My sincerest apologies, sir, but I must summon the other administrative houses in the area in order to honor this," one official stated in a slightly frightened voice. "I will need a bit of time."

"Pay me what you have. I shall gather the rest later," Nanyue replied.

"One moment please." The officials gazed at one another and then nodded in agreement. The official at the end of the table hurried into a back room, leaving Nanyue in silence.

The warrior was not known for quick thinking, intelligent though he was. He thought rather quickly now of the boy waiting outside for him. The official returned with roughly a quarter of Nanyue's payment and asked Nanyue to return the next day. The warrior nodded once to indicate understanding, gathered his payment, and returned outside to the waiting boy.

"Take me to the Yingji boarding house," Nanyue ordered.

The crowd had partially dispersed while Nanyue was in the building, and it did not reform as the two of them left the house and walked down the road. As they walked, a combination of envy and lust bubbled in Rei's stomach as his mind showed him pictures of Nanyue and some unknown female prostitute together.

Upon reaching the compound, Rei looked up at the warrior, eyes hopeful. Nanyue tossed the boy three bronze coins.

"Leave now and return at this time tomorrow." With these parting words, Nanyue turned his back and entered the building.

Rei ran home. His parents scolded him when he returned, but upon being presented with the coins as proof that the boy had been working and not fooling around, they expressed their pride to him. They were slightly upset to hear that he would be able to work the fields for only half of a day tomorrow, but were proud of Rei for finding employment with an Imperial warrior, knowing this was what he had always wanted.

By morning a note regarding the arrival of the warrior Nanyue in Jiayuguan had arrived at the administrative houses in the surrounding region. The officials in Baotou hastily composed a reply and sent it back to Jiayuguan. The note stated that they had the funds that Nanyue required there, and if he were to travel to Baotou, he could receive his remaining payment in full. That much was true; they did have a large amount of money at the Baotou Administrative House. But they had no intention of giving it to Nanyue and would rather keep it for themselves. Warriors vanished all the time, so they decided to make Nanyue and his payment vanish too.

The five hours Rei worked in the field the next morning seemed to him like eight. When it came time for him to go meet Nanyue, Rei quickly rinsed off in the washing bowl and changed his pants. As he was about to leave, Rei noticed the basket of cucumbers he had picked earlier sitting beside the house. He took two with him, thinking that Nanyue may enjoy the fresh food. Rei waited only about five minutes outside the Yingji house for Nanyue before the warrior emerged and approached the boy. Rei held out the cucumbers to Nanyue, who looked first at the food, and then at Rei.

"I thought you might enjoy some fresh food. I picked them just this morning."

Silently Nanyue accepted a cucumber. Nanyue ate the cucumber on their return to the Imperial Administrative House—something Rei noted with pleasure. They arrived at the administrative house just minutes after the note from Baotou did. The house official seemed pleased to give Nanyue the good news: he could pick up the remaining balance of his payment at once. Baotou was about a two-week ride from Jiayuguan, according to the house official, but when Nanyue told Rei he was leaving for Baotou, the boy disagreed.

"I know a quicker way to get to Baotou," said Rei. "I could take you there if you wish. We could use my pony to allow us to get there even quicker."

"Be here at sunrise, and give this to your parents as compensation for your absence." From his pocket Nanyue withdrew a large amount of money, more than Rei had ever seen in his life. His parents would be able to buy a new pony and hire somebody to work for two years with the sum.

Rei's mother sobbed a little upon hearing the news that her son would be leaving, and his father was grim; however, they both knew it was not only for the best, but was what the boy wanted as well. Rei knew he would miss his parents.

Rei arrived at Nanyue's camp a few minutes before sunrise, accompanied by his large pony. Before setting out on their journey, the boy approached Nanyue and offered him a large peach. Nanyue raised his eyebrows at the sight of the fruit and looked at Rei. Knowing that peaches were out of season, Nanyue asked, "Where did you get this?"

A grinning Rei replied, "That's my secret."

During their journey, Rei did the tasks he was assigned and asked no questions. He did not ask for breaks or complain. As the sun started to set, the two of them stopped for the night. Rei went out into the desert to gather firewood, while Nanyue unpacked the pony and set up the camp. When Rei returned, he passed his armload of wood to Nanyue with a small smile and went over to the pony to rub it down. Nanyue set a fire and cooked a small meal. They did not speak, but the silence was not uncomfortable; it lingered through the meal and tea until Rei spoke. The boy started to talk of warrior life that was half fantasy, a quarter legend, and a quarter reality. Nanyue sat silently, watching the fire and listening to Rei talk. The boy spoke in a cheerful tone of innocent happiness that was pleasant to hear and required no conversation, so Nanyue did not dissuade Rei from his dreams.

Rei approached the warrior, sinking to his knees beside him. He offered Nanyue a collection of lychee fruits in his cupped palms, the pink skins appearing red in the flickering firelight.

"I wanted to give these to you as a token of my admiration."

Rei looked up at the warrior shyly through his eyelashes. Nanyue looked at the boy, and then the fruit, flicking back and forth between the two.

"They taste as sweet as the love I feel for you," Rei said. "Please accept them."

Quick as a flash of lightning, Nanyue slapped Rei's hands, sending the fruit flying into the dirt, and was on his feet, glaring down at the boy. Rei looked up from the ground, eyes surprised and afraid.

"Do not be an idiot."

Rei bit his lip and looked at the ground. He took one deep shuddering breath and looked up.

"Forgive me."

He quickly looked down, but the firelight caught the flash of tears in his eyes. Nanyue watched Rei gather the fruit. They sat in silence before the fire and shared the lychee fruits between them, eating the soft, sweet fruit before they went to their mats to sleep for the rest of the night.

The next day was almost the same as the previous. Nanyue was pleased to see that they were going at the same pace. They crossed a large distance during the day, bringing them to the edge of the Altai Mountains, where they were able to camp on a cliff at the foot of the mountains. Nanyue had the camp set up and was waiting when Rei returned with the water. Nanyue did not need to say anything as Rei passed him the water bags and went directly to the pony, rubbing it down and leaving Nanyue to cook. Pleased to not have to push the boy to do his work, Nanyue went about his own. They spent the time in silence, the same as they had the evening before, and did not speak until Rei once again offered to do a small extra chore, tonight offering to sharpen Nanyue's butterfly swords.

Nanyue settled into his spot, expecting to hear another night of fantasies taking the guise of reality, and was surprised to hear a request instead.

"Would you please tell me of the battle of the Ugasi plains? I've heard so many different stories and legends, all of them wonderful, but I'd like to know which one is real."

Surprised by the request, Nanyue was even more surprised to find himself talking. Nanyue said their commander was killed in an earlier battle, which left him in charge. By the time they had reached the Ugasi plains, the Imperial court was desperate and promised Nanyue via their local administrators that he would be rewarded for his success. Nanyue explained to Rei his idea to dig holes to hide archers in the tall grass and how he taught them to make a high, reedy chirrup noise to communicate with each other. Nanyue told of how he was able to draw the enemy into the center of the battlefield, causing them to think they had outnumbered the few of his men who were retreating in front of them, only to be ambushed on all sides as the archers closed in from behind. Nanyue found pleasure in this act of retelling his stories.

After telling his tale, Nanyue grew silent and reflective. Rei finished with the blades and crossed around the fire to give them to the warrior for inspection. After examination, Nanyue declared the blades satisfactory and turned back to the fire. Instead of turning into the night to put away the butterfly swords, Rei approached Nanyue again. As he did the night before, Rei knelt down beside Nanyue. When Nanyue turned to look at him, Rei met his eye and withdrew a red silk box from his pocket and offered it to Nanyue.

"I have this for you," Rei said simply.

Nanyue took the box from the boy, curious as to what sort of gift he would place in such a lovely box. The silk was soft and slippery against his rough fingers. The lid slid off with no difficulty to reveal a flower against the white silk interior. The flower was red and seemed to almost foam from the branches, appearing full, light, and incredibly delicate: they were the blossoms of the rheum plant.

Nanyue looked at Rei, and then down at the flower. Nanyue tipped the flower into his hand and tossed it from the cliff. Returning the box to Rei, Nanyue left the fire for his mat, unsurprised to not hear Rei approach his mat for quite some time.

When Rei did finally go to his mat, he did not rest well. His mind was still ablaze with the devastation and humiliation from Nanyue's rejection; he was saddened by it. He did sleep eventually, his exhaustion winning over all else. Rei did not sleep well though. As he slept, he dreamed of sitting alone on the edge of a cliff. Despair seemed to run through his very veins, a crippling depression wrapping tighter and tighter around his heart. Rei decided he would jump off the cliff and end all of the agony. He looked down over the cliffs and was horrified to see the water as intermingled colors of ebony and crimson that came together but never mixed. The waves crashed against the rocks, and as Rei prepared to jump, two things happened almost at once. He saw a flash of red that made him turn his head, and he heard Nanyue speak his name. At the sound of the warrior's voice, relief so strong and genuine surged through him like a lightning bolt. So intense was the feeling that it shattered his dream and pulled him back to reality.

Rei lay on his mat, shivering a little in the predawn darkness, looking through the thin ground fog to Nanyue, who lay roughly five feet away. In the weak light Rei studied Nanyue's face, memorizing its every line, the sweep of his eyelid, the curve of his jaw. It soon became clear that sleep was no longer an option, so Rei decided to rise, thinking that Nanyue would enjoy waking to a warm breakfast. The fog did not pass by the time Nanyue and Rei had packed up and started on the road again. The day was overcast and threatening rain, but Nanyue was sure they would reach Baotou within two days' time.

Rei was quieter than usual; the details of the dream had departed but had also left an ominous feeling that he seemed unable to shake. Regardless, he was no less effective than usual, and Nanyue did not notice anything amiss as they moved along.

As the evening approached, rain seemed inevitable, so the two decided they would set up camp in a cave to keep dry. As Nanyue unpacked the pony and set up camp, he noticed Rei seemed to be taking longer than usual to fetch the wood. But it was not long after that Rei returned, arms filled with wood, banishing the boy's temporary tardiness from Nanyue's mind.

The evening passed as all the others, a comfortable schedule that Nanyue found himself getting used to. They sat in silence as they prepared and ate dinner, and then spoke as Rei repaired tatters in their clothing.

After completing his repairs, Rei left the fire. Nanyue sat up longer, half expecting Rei to return with a gift or treat. After a fair amount of time had passed, it became clear this was not going to be the case, and Nanyue felt some disappointment; he had grown used to the boy's surprises. So Nanyue too departed for his mat.

The next afternoon Nanyue and Rei were within sight of Baotou. As they approached the city, Nanyue stopped, looking ahead. There was a group of men standing across the road; they were local peacekeepers with peasant weapons. Sensing danger, Nanyue indicated to Rei that they should walk slower and approach the men openly.

"You are the warrior Nanyue?" the man in the middle of the line asked when the two had come close enough. Nanyue dipped his head in acknowledgment. Without a word, men were suddenly all over him, beating him aggressively as two men tied Rei's hands behind his back. Nanyue put up a struggle, as he was quite strong. It took some time, but the men soon restrained Nanyue as well and forced him and Rei onto horses. They took them into town and directly to the Imperial House without a single word of explanation.

Upon reaching the house, the men pulled Nanyue and Rei from the horses and forced them into the house. The Baotou house was far grander than the Jiayuguan house, floored in deep carpet with more paintings and hangings, with bronze lanterns set every few feet to keep the room illuminated.

"Warrior Nanyue, you have been brought here to be charged with theft and attempted theft from the Imperial government. We have received evidence that you presented a note at the Jiayuguan house that entitled you to funds far beyond the ones you were deemed to receive. We also have evidence that you accepted funds from the house official there, who was too terrified to refuse you. You and your accomplice are to be jailed immediately until further notice," said the Baotou house administrator.

Pulled by the restraints around their wrists, Nanyue and Rei were led down the street to the local jail and shoved into a cell. After they were securely locked in, the jailer removed their restraints through the bars and left them to themselves. The jail cell was small, damp, and dirty. The stone walls sweated tiny beads of moisture, and the two sodden mats on the floor were a uniform brown and black from the filth. Nanyue sat on the mat and looked at the wall. Rei sank down to the mat beside him, looking up into the warrior's unreadable face. Looking down, Rei saw that the ropes had cut into Nanyue's wrists, leaving angry red marks that would turn into large purple bruises. Rei wrapped his hands around the warrior's wrists, massaging them slowly and carefully. Nanyue glanced over at the boy, but his face stayed blank and unreadable. Rei massaged both of his wrists in silence. As he began to move behind the warrior, Nanyue pushed him away.

"I know that things are bad, but you don't need to worry," Rei said. "I don't know if you feel it, but we are lucky. Nothing will stay wrong, and I will support you until everything becomes right."

The warrior seemed to relax with his touch, so Rei carried on with the massage, moving back around to Nanyue's front so he could rub down his arms.

At sunrise three guards entered the cell and pulled Rei from Nanyue. He was taken out of town and threatened with torture if he returned. The guards then returned to the prison for Nanyue. The officials deliberated his fate for several weeks. They finally decided that Nanyue was to be charged with high treason and sentenced to death. The guards bound him with chains, wrapping them securely around his wrists, before escorting him to a cart to take him to his execution.

It was a long journey with many days' worth of travel. Nanyue was left in the back of the cart, lying face down on the wooden planks for the entire journey. Thinking was one of the things Nanyue did best while in prison, and he thought a lot while he lay in the cart, being driven to his death. He thought of his time with Rei, of how the boy had worked to gain his approval even after being rejected so cruelly and frequently. His face flamed with embarrassment over his actions, his stomach hollow with remorse. Nanyue found himself wishing furiously that he could change things, that he could thank Rei and show him proper appreciation. It had been a long time since Nanyue had felt lonely.

It was evening when they reached the execution site. As they pulled him from the back of the cart, Nanyue caught a look at the place he was to die in. His eyes fixed on a black spot on the ground—the faint remains of a campfire. There were new spouts, but he recognized the site. As he looked around more carefully, he recognized his exact location—it was the campsite where Rei had given him the flower.

It was the flower of the rheum plant that occupied his mind in that moment. Chains clanking, Nanyue was taken to the side of the cliff and pushed over without a word. Nanyue closed his eyes, mind clear, preparing to no longer exist when the fall stopped. A jolt of agony ripped through his arms and shoulders, but he was still far above the waves. Looking up, Nanyue could hardly believe his eyes. The chain between his wrists had snagged on the strong stalk of a plant growing from the cliff. A red rheum plant had stopped his fall, and Nanyue had no doubt that he had just experienced the luck that Rei had spoken of in the prison cell.

Hanging there was pure agony, but Nanyue kept silent so the men above him would think he was dead. He found himself fading in and out of consciousness at irregular intervals. As night fell and became morning, Nanyue started shouting out for Rei, but a sudden wind caused him to sway and awaken to find it was a dream.

As the sun started to rise, Nanyue thought he heard something. He was unsure of the noise; the wind and water had combined with his pain to create many sounds, but he was sure he had heard a person. Listening closely, he confirmed his thoughts.

"Nanyue!"

It was Rei. Nanyue felt no shock at all. He felt deep pleasure.

"Rei!"

Looking up, Nanyue saw Rei's face appear as he bent over the cliff's edge. "Fetch a rope and a hook! Catch the chains and pull me up!" Rei did not reply, but immediately vanished, leaving Nanyue with no doubt that he had run to do what he was told.

Nanyue's consciousness wavered, but he forced himself to stay awake. He watched as Rei returned and started lowering a thick rope that was knotted around an iron hook. It clanged against the stone and clinked when it hit the iron of the chain. With a small amount of jiggling, the hook went neatly through a link in the chain. Rei vanished from sight, and several seconds later, Nanyue started to rise up the side of the cliff. The motion was very jerky; the added strain to his arms caused Nanyue such intense agony that he lost consciousness once more.

When he came to, he was lying on the ground, his arms free but buzzing with pain, and his head on Rei's thigh. The young boy looked down at him with fear and happiness.

"Nanyue! What happened?"

The warrior did not reply immediately. He knew there would be talk, a lot of it from him, but for the moment he stayed silent, marveling over his unlikely rescue and planning their next move. Rei allowed him to think before taking Nanyue back to his camp, and as Nanyue spoke, Rei once again massaged the warrior; this time

Nanyue allowed it. Rei started with his back, and moved to his arms and chest. Rei slept in Nanyue's embrace when night fell.

In the morning they traveled once again. They no longer had Rei's pony, but they still moved at a speed that impressed Nanyue. It took them only a month to reach Ningsia. Rei had never been to Ningsia, but he had heard people passing through Jiayuguan speak of the place. It was a fair but honest city, and as Nanyue spoke to the officials at the government house, their eyes grew wide with horror and anger. Rei stood with Nanyue to offer his own testimony. The officials sent out notices to summon his fellow warriors; the so-called officials of Baotou would not go unpunished. They asked Nanyue if he wished to join his fellow warriors. Nanyue declined.

"I wish only for my funds and to return to the road."

With these words they hastened to gather the remainder of the payment. Upon receiving it, Nanyue rested his hand on Rei's shoulder and left the building with him.

Outside dark had fallen, the air cool and damp. Nanyue let his hand fall from Rei's shoulder, and the boy turned to him.

"I am fortunate to have you." Nanyue looked into Rei's eyes as he spoke, wanting to state this once and wanting it to be clear. "All of this money is mine, and as of now, what is mine is yours. I will do right by you from now on and care for you as you have cared for me."

A tear welled up in Rei's left eye and raced down his cheek. He smiled and wrapped his arms around the warrior, holding him in a tight embrace. Stepping back, Rei followed Nanyue as the two of them walked from the government house and into their new lives.

4 THE GAME OF NARD (PERSIA-IRAN)

In the kingdom of Persia, there once lived a great prince named Armand, whose father was the great king of the Achaemenids. He gained the trust of his people through fairness and faith.

When Prince Armand was a young man, he was sent away to learn the teachings of the great Zoroaster. When he arrived at the school, he met a happy-go-lucky student name Ravashe. Ravashe was the smartest student in the school, and all who knew him were impressed by his intelligence. Armand, too, soon grew to admire him. The one remarkable thing about Ravashe was that he was always happy. When Armand had a problem, Ravashe was always happy to help. There was never a problem Ravashe could not solve.

"Why are you always happy, Ravashe?" asked the prince.

"Because I can help you, my prince, and helping you makes me most happy," replied Ravashe.

The prince thought for a while and came back to Ravashe.

"I see that you are always giving, and it seems to please you."

"Yes, it does. And you will find that if you help me, you'd be pleased too."

"And how can I help you?" asked the prince.

Ravashe walked over to the prince, leaned in, and whispered, "Lay with me."

Upon hearing such nonsense, Prince Armand pushed Ravashe away and yelled, "You are stupid and silly, and now you tease me!" which made Ravashe roar with even more laughter.

Weeks passed and the scholarly work became heavy. Prince Armand needed Ravashe's help but did not want to be teased. So he had another student send Ravashe a note. It read:

Ravashe,

I need your help with my work, but I don't want to be teased again.

Do you promise not to tease me?

Signed,

Armand

Armand soon got his reply:

Armand,

I did not tease you. I have lectures until late, but please come with your problems and we'll work together.

Ravashe

Armand arrived that night with his problems in his hand. Instead of getting a quick reply, Ravashe hammered at the questions all night long. By the time they were finished, Armand was so tired that he could not make it back to his quarters.

"Why don't you lie here?" said Ravashe.

Tired and remembering Ravashe's promise not to tease him, Armand agreed and was welcomed into Ravashe's bed.

"Thank you," said Ravashe. He leaned in and kissed Armand.

The kiss was so soft and gentle that it made Armand realize it wasn't a joke. Soon the two were making passionate love.

After that night, Ravashe and Armand were inseparable. One day Armand was setting up a game.

"What is that?" asked Ravashe.

"It's a game called Nard," said Armand. "Would you like to learn how to play it?"

Ravashe agreed, and they were soon playing; however, the game took a very long time to play. Each night, they would play until late, and Armand would always be too tired to return to his quarters, so he would lie with Ravashe. Before long, Ravashe became quite skilled at the game of Nard. With his confidence high, he would challenge other students who also knew the game. Ravashe would often win.

Armand did not feel bad because he knew that together they were happy.

Soon word got out that Armand was doing well and that he was a close companion of the smartest scholar at the school. So the king decided he would surprise his son and pay him a visit. When the king arrived early one morning, he proceeded directly to his son's quarters; he was surprised when he found his bed empty. Naturally, he asked a student to lead him to Ravashe.

"Perhaps he'll know where my son is," he thought.

So the king was led to Ravashe's chambers, where he met Ravashe, who smiled and bowed before his king in honor.

"Ravashe, I heard you are a great companion of my son."

"Ah, yes, he is asleep here," replied Ravashe. He led the king to the prince, who was sleeping naked in Ravashe's bed.

"What is this?" demanded the king, waking Armand.

"It is love," answered Ravashe. "Your son and I are in love."

"Did you fill his head with such stupidity?" questioned the king angrily.

The king turned to his son and asked, "Is this true?"

"Yes, Father, it is," said the prince. "We are in love."

"It is forbidden," said the king. "It's against the teachings of Ahura Mazda, the supreme god!"

The king, not wanting to be made a fool, had Ravashe arrested and thrown in prison.

While in prison, Ravashe was visited by Armand,

which made him very happy.

"Well, hello, my beloved. Come sit with me," Ravashe said while smiling.

"How can you be so happy when the king wants you dead?"

"Because you stood up and told your father that you love me. That made me so happy," said Ravashe.

Armand felt that he had to save Ravashe, but how would he do it? He felt the only way was to challenge his father to a duel to the death.

"Are you good at duels?" asked Ravashe.

"No, but I'll try."

This answer sent Ravashe into a fit of laughter. He reminded Armand that he was an intelligent person and that there must be another way. However, Armand insisted. He was about to leave to go battle his father when Ravashe stopped him.

"Why don't you challenge him to something you are skilled in doing?" suggest Ravashe. "How about you challenge him to a game of Nard?"

Armand thought this to be a wonderful idea and set off to find his father.

He explained to his father that Ravashe was the most intelligent person in all of Persia and to kill him would mean a great loss to progress and science. He offered to prove this by playing a game of Nard with the most skilled player the king could find.

"Father, if I win, Ravashe goes free."

His father agreed and soon sent notice across all the land to find the greatest Nard player. The king's own advisor, the high priest Eliashib, answered the call.

"I am the only player who can defeat your son," said Eliashib.

This pleased the king, because he knew Eliashib was a wise man.

So the challenge was set: Eliashib and Armand would play. Ravashe was brought up from the prison to witness the game. Armand played heroically and quickly defeated Eliashib, surprising the entire court.

Eliashib, realizing this would potentially hurt his status, turned to the king and said, "This mere game should not be judge and jury of such a horrible act between these men. Do not anger the gods, dear king. Leave Ravashe's fate to the heavens."

Hearing this, Armand boldly stepped forward and

proclaimed, "But I won, Father! This was the agreement."

However the king saw the high priest's statement as more valid. Ignoring his son's request, the king turned to Eliashib and asked, "You are so wise. What would the gods propose we do, high priest?"

"Let me ask the gods, and I will have an answer for all of you."

The next day the king brought Ravashe out for a public trial. Knowing that he was the king of fairness, he made sure his board of governors, the school's high priests, and his entire kingdom were present. Armand was ordered to stand by his father's side during the procession. Unfazed by this public trial, Ravashe emerged, always smiling, and blew a kiss to his nervous beloved.

"Before us stands Ravashe, our school's most intelligent scholar. But as we all now see, he is not intelligent at all. He is weakened by the love of another man. The teachings of the Yasna and our ways forbid men to lie with men as they lie with women."

Ravashe smiled and said, "With all due respect, your highness, I have memorized the Yasna, and I know that it is not written."

The king turned to his board of governors, who in turn went to the high priest, who agreed with Ravashe.

"These words are not in our laws or spiritual teachings," whispered the high priest.

Not wanting to be embarrassed, the king said, "Then we shall ask Ahura Mazda directly. Our high priest shall pray to Ahura Mazda for the answer."

"You are the king of fairness, are you not?" asked Ravashe. "If you lay my fate directly before Ahura Mazda, then do so where Ahura Mazda will show all in a righteous manner."

"How do you mean, boy?" asked the high priest.

"Take two pieces of papyrus," Ravashe said. "On one write, 'LIFE;' On the other, 'DEATH.' Seal them, and let me choose my fate before everyone, handed down by Ahura Mazda."

The crowd applauded at Ravashe's statement, eager to see their god's work themselves.

The king was about to object when the high priest whispered into his ear, "Let him have his way. The notes will be sealed. We shall write 'DEATH' upon both notes."

The king nodded in agreement, but unbeknown to

him, the conversation was overheard by his son, whom the King made stay by his side.

"Very well. We shall all return here tomorrow to see our god's words," said the king.

Ravashe was returned to his prison cell. Armand came again to visit his beloved.

"Oh, I was so proud of you. Surely you must be happy that you beat the priest."

However, Armand could not share in the happiness, instead explaining his father's treachery.

"Still you smile, and I am crying. Ravashe, have you no fear?"

"If fear were a proper emotion, I would use it; but now is not the time for fear," Ravashe replied. "You are with me. I am happy. Armand, do not fight with your father. Let me take care of this myself."

Armand was so tormented that he went to his father.

"Father, this is not honest; I heard the high priest. I won't fight you on this, but at least allow me one last night with Ravashe."

"I will grant your foolish wish only because he shall be dead tomorrow. After that, we will never speak of this again," said the king.

With those words, Armand rushed to the prison to see a happy Ravashe singing love songs.

"Ravashe, this is our last night together. Tomorrow you shall be put to death once the note is read!"

"And if I live, can I have a lifetime of love with you, Armand?" Ravashe happily replied.

Armand grew angry. "Why do you tease me when you are about to die?"

Ravashe laughed. "You accused me of teasing you before, right?"

Armand admitted that he had been wrong, but this time he was certain he was right.

"Then give me your promise that if I shall live, you will give me your love for the rest of our lives. If not, you'll have our wondrous love tonight to remember."

"I promise," said Armand, "but I will love you tonight with tears in my eyes. I am sorry."

That night they made passionate love.

In the morning Ravashe was presented before the entire Persian people with two sealed notes in front of him. Ravashe blew a kiss to Armand, who was again standing next to his father and the high priest. Ravashe took the note, held it up to the sky, and shouted for all to hear:

"To beloved Ahura Mazda! I accept your fate in this note and shall make it part of me as you so proclaimed!"

He then quickly ate the note. The priest rushed to Ravashe, but he was too late—the note had been swallowed before he could reach him.

"Now, high priest, please read to all what Ahura Mazda has not chosen."

The priest picked up the note and read these words: "The death of Ravashe is just, for his love is unholy."

Ravashe and Armand lived happily ever after.

5 THE KURI VILLAGE (AUSTRALIA)

Many, many years ago, there was a land of sacred forests and meadows where soft breezes whispered to the wildflowers and birds. Here resided the Kuri people. Their ways seem simple to us today, but life was good.

One of the traditions of the Kuri people was the Fertility Solstice Festival held at the beginning of each summer. The festival included many activities, including music, plentiful foods, and games. The festival was particularly exciting because young folks of the proper age for mating were permitted to select their partner after partaking in games that fully demonstrated their skills and talents.

One particular year, it so happened that the Kuri people had eleven young folks all at the proper age for coupling: six males and five females. The chief of the Kuri people at that time was an unpopular, arrogant, overbearing bully. It was through him that each couple would be chosen. So he announced that he would select the partners in marriage, and that prior to permitting them to wed, each of the eleven young folks would be required to select one skill from a list of eleven in which to demonstrate their full expertise during the games.

Of the young men, Tartak selected hunting as the skill in which he would demonstrate his expertise. Sire picked running and practiced by running the news between the villages of the other tribes. Airon chose fishing, spending many enjoyable hours each day catching delicious fish. Silon decided on building, honing his skill by improving the homes of many of the Kuri people. Pale picked climbing, a skill he developed by picking fruits and nuts hidden high up in the trees. Finally, Minar chose knife throwing. He didn't know too much about knife throwing, but it was the only remaining skill listed for the young men.

Minar worked on his knife throwing closely with Tartak, the hunter. He did this because Tartak was good with a spear, which closely resembled the knives used for throwing. The two would go hunting together, often disappearing for days at a time. Soon a special friendship developed between the young men, and they became best friends. Invariably the two returned with wonderful bounties of tasty meats. Their skills improved rapidly, because the wild beasts were plentiful in those days.

The young women were sent off to a secret location nearby where they could privately hone their skills and wears. Airmia selected tanning as the skill she would develop. Shelaya, the daughter of the village medicine man, focused on medicine. Lare, the daughter of the chief, chose painting. Zaleshe chose farming. Silo, knowing that measuring was an important skill for the tribe, chose pieced measuring as her skill.

Finally the day of the Solstice Festival arrived. Silon was chosen to go first in demonstrating his expertise in his skill. He showed a balance scale he had built that tipped from side to side. The chief paired Silon with Airmia. Airmia said the scale would be great to divvy up food portions. Airmia, who earlier had skinned two goats and tanned their hides, displayed a very nice set of clothing for Silon, who was thoroughly pleased. Everyone cheered as Silon and Airmia walked off, hand in hand.

Minar was next. His chosen mate was Lare. Lare, spoiled by the privileges of being the chief's daughter, ordered Minar to perform a stunt that was particularly special. But Minar was unable to think of a special way to throw a knife to please her. Angered by his lack of creativity, Lare told him to throw the knife as high as he could into the sky. Hoping to please her, Minar obliged; however, he had never practiced throwing his knife straight up and was not skilled at it. But up went the knife, far into the sky. When it finally came down, it sliced into Lare's toe! The chief was absolutely outraged and immediately beat poor Minar until he was almost unconscious. The entire village looked on in shock, but out of fear they said nothing. The other young men carried the badly beaten Minar to the tribal lodge.

While the other young men returned to the festival site, Tartak, the hunter, remained behind to care for his friend, Minar. Before long, the arrogant chief sent Sire, the runner, to order Tartak to leave Minar to die and return to the festival. Tartak sent Sire back to the chief with the message that he would not return because he must care for Minar. The chief was angered and sent Sire back to Tartak with another message:

If you don't return to the festival, you will be banished immediately! Both you and Minar must be out of the village by sundown!

By now, Tartak was very angered by the chief's actions and words. Fearing the consequences, Sire pleaded with his friend to obey. But Tartak pledged that he would not leave his best friend.

Understanding the dilemma, Sire told Tartak, "My friend, we have known each other our entire lives. While you hunted the land, I spent time running the trails for many years. I know the land better than anyone. I know some secrets. If you follow the summer sun to where it sleeps, you will come upon a hidden trail. This trail will take you to an unknown valley. Make a new home there. The valley is safe and is plentiful in everything you will need."

Tartak quickly fashioned a tilt sled, placed Minar on it, and hurriedly set off toward the solstice sunset and the unknown valley. It was long into the night when Tartak found the valley. Worn out from dragging Minar and the sled so far, he set up camp near a bubbling stream. Without provisions, Tartak cupped his hands to get water for himself and Minar. He pulled some branches over them under a young lancewood tree and went to sleep. It had been a rough afternoon and night, but they made it, completely exhausted.

Awakening to the sound of rustling nearby, Tartak and Minar were relieved to find Silon and his new mate, Airmia, approaching.

"Sire told us where you would be, and we wanted to help," explained Silon.

Airmia had brought some new clothes she had made from her animal skins. Silon quickly put together a simple shelter to protect Tartak and Minar from the elements. While Silon worked, Airmia watched over Minar, allowing Tartak to catch some small animals for a good meal. Minar was still very weak and needed more rest, but his injuries were already healing. In fact, he had the energy to eat and talk. Near the day's end, Airmia and Silon said good-bye and headed back to the Kuri village. Tartak and Minar were again alone for the night.

The second morning in the hidden valley, Tartak and Minar were again jolted awake by a nearby noise. Suddenly Airon and Shelaya appeared. Shelaya had brought some herbs and homemade ointments she knew would help heal Minar's injuries. As she tended to Minar's wounds, Airon told Tartak to rest while he went and caught enough fish for at least two days. After a big fish dinner, Shelaya explained how to apply the ointments and herbs, and left a pouch containing a powder of dried herbs to be taken each day with water. She said that in the quiet valley with the clear air and clean water, Minar would heal more each day and would soon be up and about. As the end of the day neared, Airon and Shelaya bid their farewells and left, heading back to the village.

No new visitors came to the valley for the next few days. Minar and Tartak's days were filled with activities such as setting up their new home and hunting for more food.

Minar looked at Tartak and said, "I feel sad that you did not get a mate because of me."

Tartak confessed that he was glad it had all happened, because after the years they spent together, he felt unable to take a female mate; he hoped that Minar would accept him as his mate. Minar was happy at these words and accepted. It was their first night making love.

A few days passed, and Pale arrived with his new mate, Zaleshe. Zaleshe brought more clothing, fresh vegetables from her garden, spices for cooking, and some seeds. She also showed Tartak and Minar the best spot in the hidden valley for a productive garden. Pale spent the day climbing trees in the valley to harvest rich fruit and nuts. After a wonderful vegetarian meal, it was time for Pale and Zaleshe to return to the village.

About a week later, Sire returned, this time with his new mate, Silo. Silo measured out the tools and supplies that Tartak and Minar would need to get them through the winter. As Sire showed them other trails in the hidden valley, the two hunters bagged more than enough game for a big dinner. As the months of summer continued on, various friends from the Kuri village took turns visiting Tartak and Minar in the hidden valley.

But one day there was a shock. Lare, the spoiled daughter of the village chief, arrived with her new mate from another village. Lare told them her unpopular father had died in his sleep. The chief had never been the same after his outbursts of rage against Minar and Tartak. The anger and unwillingness to forgive was believed to have weakened his arrogant heart beyond repair. Lare went on to explain that her father had forbidden anyone from any further contact with Minar or Tartak. But she realized that holding a grudge, especially an unwarranted one, was no way to go through life; it was not the way of the Kuri people.

Lare said she would have come sooner, but her foot had not healed. She told them that she had coordinated all of the visits to the hidden valley and that she strongly admired the mind-set of Minar and Tartak to be courageous, not hold grudges, and willingly move on with their lives. Lare had learned a valuable lesson in life from Minar and Tartak, one she had not learned from her father—to be courageous, but also to be humble and peaceful. Lare also invited Minar and Tartak to return to the village before the bitter winter set in. They did, and the Kuri people continued to live peacefully for many more years.

6 TUKKURUQ AND UQUITCHUQ: THE STORY OF NIGHT AND DAY (CANADA)

Long, long ago, when the world was still new, the Inupiat people lived in the dark north. They were a hunting people, and none was fiercer than Tukkuruq. He was not only the fiercest and smartest of the warriors, but also the most handsome. He had eyes like the wolf, skin like a ghost, and hair as dark as the raven. He was known for his dark blue cloak that he wore while hunting. His cloak's color was of great importance because the tribe lived in constant darkness and his light skin was easy to spot, especially while hunting.

The north had many nomad tribes known as bands. They wandered through the darkness and would often meet. One day a particular band came to the Inupiat people for help. Their hunters had poor vision and were often killed. This particular nomad tribe was made up of mostly women. Tukkuruq was offered several women from the tribe, but he wanted none.

One of the tribe's women was named Karima. She came to Tukkuruq and said, "I know you are smart. I am too. I can tell you about something you don't know."

"What is it?" he inquired.

"I can tell you about Light. He helps you see and brightens the area around you. But I won't say any more."

Tukkuruq lay awake thinking about her words.

The next day he came to her with food for her and her family. So she told him, "In brightness, everything grows. You don't always have to hunt, but I will say no more."

"Why not?" asked Tukkuruq.

She made Tukkuruq an offer. "I want you to tell the band you chose me for your mate," she said.

Tukkuruq refused.

"Am I not to your liking?"

Tukkuruq offered to bring her food and animal hides to make clothing, but she still refused to divulge her secrets. When his curiosity got the best of him, he finally asked her what he could do to hear more from her about Light.

"Lie with me until I am with child," she said.

So each night he lay with her, and just before they went to sleep, she told him more about Light. They lay together until she became pregnant. Karima was happy to be carrying the child of the finest hunter of the north.

One day she told Tukkuruq the precise location where Light existed.

"Twelve thousand wingbeats south of the polar star, you will find Uquitchuq," she said.

"Uquitchuq is the place?" Tukkuruq asked.

"No, Uquitchuq is the man. He brings Light."

So Tukkuruq went to the medicine man of the band and asked him to brew a potion that would turn him into a bird.

"Why would you want to be a bird?" asked the medicine man. "You have the eyes of a wolf, the beauty of a man, and the skin of a ghost."

Tukkuruq explained his search for brightness and Light as told by Karima. The medicine man was also wise and always put his people's needs first.

"Tukkuruq, you are selfish and think only of yourself. You do not take a mate, you share only when asked, and you give only when given. If I make you into this bird, you must bring this Light back to your people."

Tukkuruq promised and was given the potion to turn him into a bird. Now a bird, Tukkuruq flew for many miles through the never-ending dark of the north, following the exact path and instructions as told by Karima. He grew weary many times and almost turned back. But at last he saw a rim of light at the very edge of the horizon and knew that the daylight was close. Tukkuruq strained his wings and flew with all his might. Suddenly the daylight world burst upon him with all its glory and brilliance. The endless shades of color and the many shapes and forms surrounding him made Tukkuruq stare and stare. He flapped down to a tree and rested, exhausted by his long journey.

Above him the sky was an endless blue, the clouds fluffy and white. Tukkuruq could not get enough of the wonderful scene. Eventually Tukkuruq lowered his gaze and realized that he was near a village that lay beside a wide river. As he watched, a beautiful man with great muscles, tan skin, and golden hair came to the river near the tree in which he was perched. He dipped a large bucket into the icy waters of the river and then turned to make his way back to the village.

Tukkuruq flew down and spoke to the handsome man.

"What is your name?" asked Tukkuruq.

The handsome man was startled and looked up at the darkest bird he had ever seen. It was tall and had glowing eyes. Scary though it was, the man was fascinated because a bird had never spoken to him before.

"I am Uquitchuq," replied the man.

"Do you live in Light?"

Uquitchuq laughed. "But of course! In fact, I am the keeper of Light for our village."

"Great," said Tukkuruq. "Can I rest on your shoulder and return with you to the village?"

Uquitchuq was a delightful fellow and thought how thrilled everyone would be to see the talking bird. He naturally agreed. So Tukkuruq carefully climbed onto Uquitchuq's shoulder. Together they returned to the snow lodge of Uquitchuq's father, the chief of the village people.

"OK."

"Promise me."

"I promise."

It was warm and cozy inside the lodge. Tukkuruq looked around and spotted a box that glowed around the edges. "Light," he thought to himself. Tukkuruq knew he had to find a way to stay so he could learn all he could from Uquitchuq in order to bring Light back to his people.

"Uquitchuq," the bird said, "I can tell you about darkness."

"Darkness? What is that?"

"It is a beautiful thing. It brings coolness and allows things to rest."

"Tell me more."

"I shan't."

"Why not?"

"Because I want you to make love to me in my human form."

Expecting a beautiful girl, Uquitchuq was shocked when the bird transformed into a striking male with a sharp red cloak.

"You tricked me!" yelled Uquitchuq. He immediately attacked Tukkuruq.

The two were of equal strength, and the battle was fought to a draw. Both men were exhausted.

Tukkuruq sighed. "You promised," he said.

Uquitchuq thought about it and felt himself a fool for not asking in advance. Plus he was curious about darkness. So he honored his promised and lay with Tukkuruq.

Afterward Tukkuruq said, "The dark is wonderful; it makes you seek in the unknown, causes you to follow your other senses, and brings glorious delight. It is cool and silent and helps in the hunt."

Delighted, Uquitchuq wanted to see this darkness for himself. But Tukkuruq had no way of taking him there because he had only enough potion left for the return trip home.

"I will tell you what. I will split the potion with you. It will be weak, so you'll only have wings. I will wait here. You will fly to our village of darkness with the ball of

Light. Tell them I sent you and then use the other half to return to me."

Uquitchuq obliged. Drinking the potion to the point where beautiful white wings sprouted from his back, Uquitchuq took a shining ball of Light and placed it in his satchel. Tukkuruq then gave Uquitchuq his cloak.

"Your journey will bring you coldness you have never known. You will need my blue cloak. However, I cannot live long in Light without it, so you must hurry back."

Uquitchuq flew off to the dark, cold north, following the path that was given to him. When he arrived at Tukkuruq's village, the people looked at him in amazement. Uquitchuq enjoyed the darkness and the people around him. He thought it better than Light and was determined to stay. When he went to ask the elders for acceptance into their band, the medicine man noticed the blue cloak belonging to Tukkuruq.

"I have come to be among you," pleaded Uquitchuq.

"And why should we allow this?"

"Because I bring you this!" With those words he reached into his satchel and brought out Light. All looked on in awe and wonder.

"All right," said the elders. "Let him join us."

"Let him join us!" cheered the members of the band.

"Wait!" exclaimed the wise medicine man. "Who told you of darkness?" he asked.

It was then that Uquitchuq remembered his promise to return to Tukkuruq.

Uquitchuq confessed that it was Tukkuruq and pleaded with the medicine man.

"I have been selfish, oh great one. Have pity on me and help me save Tukkuruq, for he is surely weak without his cloak."

The medicine man made a potion that would allow Tukkuruq to return, and he gave Uquitchuq some medicine to make Tukkuruq better.

"You owe him both for sending you here and for staying too long."

"What shall I do?" said Uquitchuq, who was saddened by his selfishness.

"That I cannot tell you. Ask Tukkuruq how you can repay him."

So Uquitchuq took the potion and flew back to his village of Light.

Tukkuruq was weak and near death when Uquitchuq arrived. Uquitchuq nursed Tukkuruq for many weeks until he was well again.

"I am sorry," said Uquitchuq. "I marveled in your world too long at your expense. How can I repay you?"

Tukkuruq looked at Uquitchuq and said, "Look into your heart and come to me freely."

With that Uquitchuq looked into his heart and thought of the love Tukkuruq gave to him, the rich darkness that he shared, and how he missed him.

"You opened me up to your world as I did to you. I will give you my heart. Our love isn't of your village or of mine, but rather ours." Then he rubbed the remaining potion onto Tukkuruq's back, giving them both wings. They flew up into the sky and lived happily ever after.

All the people exclaimed their happiness and good fortune due to the love of Tukkuruq and Uquitchuq. To reward them, Tukkuruq and Uquitchuq take turns waving to the world. When Tukkuruq waves, night falls. When Uquitchuq waves back the light comes upon that part of earth again.

7 THE BLUE DOOR (RUSSIA)

голубой дверь

Once upon a time, there lived a Tzar who had three sons. His first and eldest son was destined to be the next Tzar. His second son was destined to head the military. His youngest son, Prince Evgenii, was to be in charge of the country's finances.

When the three sons came of age, the Tzar proclaimed "Arrow Day" to be a special day, a day when his sons could roam freely and shoot their arrows into the door of the homes of whom they wished to marry. The Tzar was wise and wanted his subjects to admire him. So, he proclaimed that on "Arrow Day", anyone chosen by his sons would be permitted to marry. This gave hope to non-noble subjects, as it was a chance for their daughters to marry into royalty.

Now the two older princes were very talented with the bow and arrow. Prince Evgenii, however, was not so sure of his ability. He was worried that he would embarrass his family by not shooting well. So, Evgenii decided that he would wake up early at daybreak and practice in the farm fields.

After practicing day after day in the farm fields, he felt he was making no progress towards improving his skill. He felt hopeless. Luckily, he was noticed by a farmhand of his same age working in the fields, who one day came forward to offer his assistance. Prince Evgenii welcomed his help, and soon the two became close friends. Every morning at sunrise they would meet and practice. This went on for several weeks.

One morning, the farmhand did not show up until late, when the prince had to leave. The farmhand's hands and clothes were covered in blue paint. The prince was angry and yelled at the farmhand. The farmhand apologized, and explained that he needed to make up for the time lost in training the prince—he had other chores he needed to do to help provide for his family.

Prince Evgenii felt terribly guilty. The next day when they met for arrow lessons, he brought a gift of new clothes for the farmhand to wear. To the prince's surprise, the farmhand also brought the prince a gift:

fruit. They had both brought their gifts as an apology for their actions from the day before. Overjoyed, they hugged. But when they pulled back from the hug, they both kissed. It was at this moment that they realized they were in love.

Confused, Prince Evgenii did not want to continue with the arrow lessons because he did not want to pick a wife. Instead he wanted to be with the farmhand. The farmhand, knowing the prince's displeasure for embarrassment, told the prince to forget him and to continue with "Arrow Day" as planned. The prince agreed but both were very sad.

"Arrow Day" soon arrived, and the entire kingdom was excited about the event. As the three princes prepared themselves for the day, they confided in each other their choices. "We shall ride to the North" said the eldest prince. "I want to marry the daughter of the noble family that supplies our linens". The second prince said, "I will shoot my arrow into the door of the noble family to the West that supplies our kingdom with spices. I know they have two daughters and I will pick the one that suits me best." Prince Evgenii said, "I am afraid that I can't confess my love because it is forbidden. But I will tell you where we shall ride. The house will be a farm with a blue door".

Prince Evgenii's brothers had pity for him, because they thought he had erroneously picked a peasant girl to marry. "Don't worry brother, father did say ANYONE, and we will support you and whomever you decide"

So, the Tzar led the royal procession with pride, his three sons trailing behind him. First they rode to the North, where the eldest son shot his arrow into the door of the noble family that supplied the kingdom with linens. When the arrow landed, the noble family came out with their daughter Katarina. The eldest prince asked for her hand in marriage, to which she of course said yes. The crowd cheered.

The royal entourage then rode to the West, where the second son shot his arrow into the door of the noble family who supplied the kingdom with spices. Again, the family came out with their two daughters, the second son chose his mate, and the crowd applauded.

On the third journey, the royal entourage came upon a farm with a blue door. "I do not know what family lives here." said the Tzar. Prince Evgenii rose from his horse and shot his arrow into the blue door with such force and precision that all were impressed. This action brought out the farmer, his wife, and their only child, the farmhand that had helped Prince Evgenii.

The prince got off his horse and brought the farmhand to the Tzar. The Tzar looked at him in confusion. "Father, this is the person whom I wish to marry." said Prince Evgenii. The Tzar was outraged. "How dare you bring shame to your family like this!" said the Tzar. Prince Evgenii was arrested, stripped of his royal title, and sent to Siberia for punishment. Before he departed, Prince Evgenii said to the farmhand, "Please wait for me, we will be together. Just have faith."

Several years later the Tzar died, and his eldest son was proclaimed the new Tzar. The new Tzar's first order was to have his youngest brother fetched from Siberia and brought to him at one. When Prince Evgenii returned to the royal castle several months later, the new Tzar said to him, "I will restore your royal title and your honour. 'Arrow Day', as it is written and proclaimed, means you are free to marry anyone."

So the next day, the new Tzar and his two brothers rode out to find the farm again. Now, it had been several years, and they couldn't remember the way. They luckily found the farm, which they recognized by its faded blue door. However, it was not one but three arrows that landed on the door, this time shot by each of the three brothers.

The farmer, his wife, and their son came out in confusion and the new Tzar said "We welcome you into our family." With these words, Prince Evgenii got off his horse, took the hand of the farmhand, and they lived happily ever after.

And, this is why the color blue represents gay love in Russia.

8 THE PINK TIE DANCE (ARGENTINA)

The boy decided that he loved dusk the best, that time of day when the sky slowly fades into a smoky orange haze. Tourists were being ushered off old buses into the vibrant village square.

He could hear the fervent melody of guitars and the cacophonous footsteps and laughter of amateur dancers, the willing tourists only too happy to pay for a flamenco lesson. The music's magnetic rhythm pulled him closer to the center of town.

The village square was a sight to behold, now being at its fullest capacity. People were brimming over the edges of the courtyard, and strangers' elbows would occasionally collide, coupled with apologetic smiles.

Women, draped in light linen dresses, twirled and stomped to the beat, while their partners awkwardly attempted to keep up.

Though it gave him impeccable joy to see these foreigners enjoying themselves, this scene was not the reason he had come. His eyes roamed over the oscillating waves of bright textiles and sweat-shined faces, brows furrowed in concentration. Finally he located a figure dressed in pure white.

The man's onyx curls fell across his eyes as he swayed to the music. This eccentric fellow was curling his arms around his head and torso, elbows bent at an elegant angle and wrists rotating sensuously, while the snap of his fingers hit every beat of the melody. His posture was unyielding yet graceful, even in stillness.

Suddenly the man began to dance in earnest. Each movement was precise: toes and heels stomping in time to the slapping of the guitars' soundboard and the clapping of a cheering audience. The emotion of the singer's voice swelled and mingled with the dancer's passionate sway. Despite the distance, the boy could sense the performer's energy vibrating through the moist summer air like warm water lapping at his skin. When the man had finished and the music had stopped, the crowd burst into applause. Even when the dancer smiled and thanked the crowd heartily, there seemed to be a double meaning behind every expression and action outside the realm of the flamenco.

The dancer turned toward the call of his name and made his way to an acquaintance. The boy watched their casual exchange; he recognized the other male as a British tour guide who brought swarms of European tourists to this town every week.

It wasn't as if they had actually spoken to each other—this boy and Marizio—but they had exchanged a brief, silent dialogue, and Marizio's intent had been clear. Each night their eyes met, and Marizio would dip his head a fraction, hold out his hand, and make a small bow, offering a smile that was both welcoming and indifferent. An invitation. Each time this happened, the boy would turn and flee back to the fields, away from the village.

"Will you do me the honor tonight?" The graceful man extended his arm toward the boy one night, his black brow raised delicately so the boy would not run away. The boy stood motionless, neither accepting nor rejecting the invitation.

"Problem?" Marizio relaxed his arm nonchalantly back to his side.

"I can't."

"Can't…" Marizio wondered, "or won't?"

"My family works on an orchid farm. This costs too much." He spread his arms, as if to showcase his wrinkled, muddied shirt and equally filthy denim overalls. Dried mire still caked the worn out soles of his boots. "Does it look like I have the money for this?" His voice was as hard as granite, and he hissed the last word, as if joining the dance would be the most despicable thing to do.

The boy started to turn. He had embarrassed himself enough.

"I apologize." The man sounded genuine, but the boy's attention was focused solely on the fingers coiled around his wrist that stopped him from moving away. "Please..."

"What do you want from me?" the boy whispered, still looking at their linked hands. Marizio released him.

"Do you want this?" Marizio asked. Even as he indicated the dancing crowd with a nod of his head, the boy could feel another meaning hanging behind that question as Marizio gazed at him with measured intensity. The boy decided to ignore the latter sentiment and looked out longingly at the flamboyantly dressed tourists. Marizio sighed, shaking his head. "I'll pay your way."

"No," the boy replied with a glare.

Marizio could tell that this was going to be the boy's final answer. "Fine." Marizio wasn't going to waste time. "How about this: You bring me some crops from your farm as payment, and I'll give you a lesson."

The boy paused and thought for a moment. It was a fair offer. "Apples are in season."

Marizio's lips twitched with amusement. "Good." One more step brought the dancer out of the open area and into the boy's space. "Are you the serpent offering the fruit then?" His irises glimmered playfully.

"I–I'm sorry?"

"Genesis. From the Bible," Marizio said, stepping away again. The boy released a shaky breath he didn't realize he was holding. "Tomorrow midnight then."

After dinner, when his father was enjoying his pipe on the porch, the boy sneaked into his parents' room where his mother's old and battered Bible with faded silver lettering sat forgotten in a bedside drawer. Quickly he flipped to the first chapter, which informed him of the creation of the universe. Soon after he found what he was searching for. In the third chapter he learned about how the cunning serpent had successfully tempted Eve to eat fruit from the Tree of the Knowledge of Good and Evil, which God had specifically forbidden her from eating. The price was their fall and exile from the Garden of Eden.

As he walked down the deserted road toward the village with the frail crescent moon as his only company, the boy's thoughts kept returning to the fall of Adam and Eve, and what the offering of apples he had brought for Marizio—freshly picked and now bundled up securely in a cloth behind his back—could mean. The stiff material of his father's charcoal-toned shirt clung uncomfortably to his skin. It was his father's best shirt; he had no fine clothing of his own. He hadn't told his father that he was borrowing it.

The courtyard at midnight felt especially silent and empty after the boisterous festivity earlier that evening. Tendrils of smoke slithered upward from the bonfire in the middle of the yard, red embers glowing weakly. Adjacent to the dying fire stood a familiar figure, his back to the boy. Clutching the apples in his arms, the boy walked toward the shadow, his steps crisp and determined. At the dancer's feet, he placed the package of fruit.

One of the apples rolled out of the opening, and the decadent redness of its skin and the curvature of its shape had an unspeakable sensuality to it.

Marizio turned, but it was too dark to see his expression. Instead, he touched the boy's russet locks as a silent acknowledgement.

"Where's your tie?" he asked, and though his voice was soft, it sounded like an explosion of stars in the night air.

"You know I don't have one." The boy tried to control the irritation evident in his voice.

"You're angry with me again," Marizio said with a small, almost fond, smile.

"Yes." He refused to look at the man's jesting face.

"But here's my gift to you." Marizio folded the boy's collar up and slipped a piece of cloth around his neck before skillfully tying a knot. After Marizio had smoothed down his collar and stepped back, the boy carefully raised his hand, his fingers memorizing the silky texture of the tie. His eyes caught the tulip pink color under the artificial glow of streetlamps. It was a fine contrast to the gray of his shirt.

He finally had the courage to look Marizio in the eye, confusion dancing in the depths of his irises. "But I am the one to offer."

"Can we not offer each other? Come."

Before he could properly respond, Marizio drew the boy into his arms.

"But there's no music," the young man protested, trying to pull away. But Marizio's hold was firm. "I won't dance well," he warned.

"Has anybody ever told you that you worry too much?" Marizio chuckled, lowering his head right beside the boy's so their cheeks almost touched. Their bodies were still when he started to sing in a low rumble, first humming the notes and gradually blending in words. "Hay temblor de gotán…este tango es para vos…" It was a song for an upbeat tango, but with the tempo decreased, the boy found it easier to sway and follow Marizio's guiding steps.

The song seemed endless, and once he discovered the pattern of movements, the boy had an easier time following his partner. A pleased smile spread across his lips, his cheeks tinting from both exercise and exhilaration.

He couldn't recall how long he stayed with Marizio that night. Time was meaningless, but it would cruelly continue its passage. After this night, it would be a long while before he set eyes on the flamenco dancer again.

"Querido mío…"

Someone was touching his face, and he winced as he remembered the half-blossomed bruise on his jaw. "Sorry." He felt the person's hand retract and then find his own hand under the covers. His head was attempting to pound his consciousness into oblivion as he blinked against the blinding light of the room.

"Nombre de dios, what happened to you?" It was a hushed question, one that didn't demand an immediate reply, but the horror in the speaker's tone was obvious.

It was difficult to open his eyes, and he thought that staying in the cold darkness would be much more comforting. But instead of the pleasant nothingness he expected, flashes of violently vibrant colors began to wash through his mind, memories of things much more realistic: the livid red of his father's cheeks as he demanded his son's whereabouts that night and the accusatory look seething in his forest green eyes. The steely sound of their shouts, volleyed back and forth, that only concluded with a slap in the face and the promise of denunciation of their father-son relationship should he dare to return home.

He gasped at the memory of his father's anger, guilt festering beneath his skin. But still, he refused to open his eyes.

He remembered the blazing greens of orchards and the muted browns of soil roads and that eternal loop of pearl sky as raindrops dominated the weeks of summer he had spent alone, faithless, wandering on the streets with no aim but one. The incessant wet weather meant that outdoor dance lessons were cancelled and had been moved to an indoor studio.

Day after day he had walked along busy tourist-filled boulevards, searching for that familiar figure clad in white. The memory of that elegant arc of his body as he moved fluidly across the floor came back insistently, fueling him in his search. Night after night the boy wound the pink tie around his neck, the cool silky fabric soothing him as he imagined the touch of warm fingers trailing delicately upon his face and a deep voice singing sweetly in his ears.

Before long he ran out of what little money he had and found himself weak, dirty, and unwilling to get up from his resting place. Before he succumbed to welcoming darkness, the last thing he recalled was the blurry image of people's legs hurrying down the sidewalk: some bare, some nylon, some denim. As his head slowly lowered, all he could see was a field of pink.

All this he told Marizio, who had spotted his unconscious form from a local store he frequented for sundries. Marizio had taken him home without hesitation. They were now sitting side by side on Marizio's bed, sheets covering the lower halves of their bodies. Late afternoon sunlight slanted in through the blinds, and stripes of taupe and gold created a mesmerizing pattern on the cloth. Their hands were clasped together; the boy's head rested on the dancer's shoulder.

"I hate it here." The squeeze of his fingers became tighter. Marizio's thumb brushed reassuringly on the back of his hand, and he relaxed slightly.

"We could leave if you want." Marizio felt the boy's head nod yes.

"You mean, this is where we'll be living from now on?" The boy's mouth was wide open, and his childlike wonder made Marizio laugh. Their luggage had already been taken onto the cruise ship, and they had decided to head out to the dock for some fresh air before they set sail.

"Remember the day we first spoke to each other?"

The boy nodded.

"Well, a friend—he's a tour guide from a pretty big cruise ship line in Europe—offered me a position as a dance instructor on their ships. I had refused then," he explained. The boy remembered the conversation he had seen from the distance all those weeks ago.

"The room will be quite small, and the tourists might be a tad bit irksome at times if they are cooped up inside this ship for too long," Marizio told him with a grin. "But the pay is great, and we don't have to worry about food or shelter for at least a year, according to the contract."

The boy didn't comment. He breathed in the salty ocean, eyes closed for a moment to let the promise of a new and happier life wash over him.

"What are you thinking of?"

"Home," He opened his eyes again and glanced up at the man who had changed everything. "With you."

Other books by Icon Empire Press:

Visit our website: www.gaybooks.info

The Gay Icon Contemporary Short Stories by Robert
Joseph Greene

(ISBN 9780986929762)

This collection of Icon Contemporary Short Stories is a
series of male experiences to varying degrees of depth. It
looks at the gay experience with modern day living for most
of us and it connects us with a certain understanding of the
human heart.

Icon Empire Press

This High School Has Closets

(ISBN 9781927124048)

Sometimes coming out during high school just isn't an option. For Mark Thomas, finding out that he was gay falling in love, and dealing with becoming an adult, made it even tougher. High school is a challenge. "This High School Has Closets" is a story of two young teenagers falling in love during a difficult senior year.

CROSSOVER II: Straight Men – Gay Encounters

(ISBN 9781468072341)

This is the expanded print book from the successful eBook which addresses the psychological struggle men go through in dealing with their desire or curiosity with same sex encounters. CROSSOVER II: Straight Men – Gay Encounters is a collection of short stories that shows what it's like before, during and after such encounters occur.